The Far Side of the Lough

The Far Side of the Lough

Stories from an Irish Childhood

by

POLLY DEVLIN

Illustrated by Ian Newsham

LONDON
VICTOR GOLLANCZ LTD
1983

Text © Polly Devlin 1983
Illustrations © Ian Newsham 1983

British Library Cataloguing in Publication Data
Devlin, Polly
  The far side of the lough.
  I. Title   II. Newsham, Ian
  823'.912[J]   PZ7

ISBN 0-575-03244-8

Printed in Great Britain at
The Camelot Press Ltd, Southampton

*I dedicate this book to my parents
who have always lived on the near side of the lough*

Author's Note

Although these stories are fiction they are based on a real place called Ardboe and the real people who surrounded me when I was a child growing up there and who gave me through their way of life and generosity and love much of the material background of this book. To them I extend my warmest appreciation and gratitude.

Contents

The China Doll — 13

Strawberry Hearts — 35

The Pig Tree — 47

The Mad Horse — 63

The Willow-pattern Place — 77

The Charm and the Pin Tree — 91

The Petrified Stone — 105

The China Doll

The China Doll

My mother died when I was a little girl and Mary-Ellen Martin came to look after me. She had red hair, and speckled eyes and a face that was brown with freckles, and she always wore a flowery cross-over overall tied at the back, except on Sundays when she wore what she called her Costume which was a grey suit with a pleated skirt and a blouse. She wore wellingtons when she went outside the back door to feed the hens, or to get water from the pump or, when the pump broke, as it often did, to draw water up from the well.

Inside the house, in the kitchen and scullery, with their flagstone floors that she scrubbed every day, she wore plimsolls, only she called them gutties. She always went bare-legged in summer except when she was going to worship, for there were no such things as tights then and stockings were expensive.

In the winter Mary-Ellen wore men's socks and when she ran outside to feed the hens or collect eggs or to get coal or water, her legs became covered in goose-pimples which she called warbles. Whenever I was naughty she always said she'd beat me so hard she would leave my legs in warbles. But she never hit me in her life.

The thing I loved more than almost anything was for Mary-Ellen to tell me stories about when she was a little girl, the youngest of seven children and living in a two-roomed house on the shores of Lough Neagh, the biggest lake in Ireland.

The place where she lived was called Ardboe, which meant High Cow in Irish. There was an old ruined abbey there, near where she lived, and beside it a High Cross, built a thousand years before, and still standing because its mortar had been mixed with the milk of a magic cow that lived on the hill where the Cross stood. "So it was the High Cow," Mary-Ellen said, "and one bad night some bad men who coveted the cow and its magic powers came and made off with the beast and stole it away. When the monks came the next morning, there was no cow and nowhere to find it. As they were mourning the loss, they saw that on the stones, by the side of the lough, there was the imprint of the cow's hoof. They followed the markings and it led them far away to where the cow was hid, and they took her back, and finished the Cross and there it still is and if you walk up to Golloman's Point," Mary-Ellen said, "and you know where to look, you can see still the stone with a hoof mark in it, from when she left her trail."

I knew that Mary-Ellen's house was near Golloman's Point, where the charming man lived, and that it was set back from a road called the Car Road and that the lane that led to her house was called a loanin. When Mary-Ellen first told me the name of the road and I said, surprised, "But Mary-Ellen there were no cars in your day," she laughed at me saying 'your day' like that and explained that car meant any four-wheeled vehicle.

Mary-Ellen's house was small and low with thick mud walls, whitewashed every year, and a black rim painted along the bottom to hide splashes and mud marks. The roof was corrugated iron, painted bright green, and the rain, Mary-Ellen said, rattled on it as though someone was clodding stones at it. There were two rooms in the house, the kitchen and the bedroom, which Mary-Ellen always called the Room when she was telling me about it. There was no lavatory, no bathroom, and nowhere to go if you wanted to be alone. There were five beds in the bedroom and Mary-Ellen, as the smallest child, slept in the truckle bed that was kept under her parents' bed.

There was no electricity then and though they got paraffin oil lamps when Mary-Ellen was older, when she was a little girl, the same age as me, the only light for the evenings and nights were tallow candles which her mother made by dipping rushes into animal fat. They gave a flickering, dim light, but since there were no books to read, and as Mary-Ellen's sisters and mother could knit without looking at what they were doing, that frail light was not a problem.

Two or three evenings neighbours would call in for what they called a crack – an evening's talk, sitting around the flickering fire in the half-light, telling ghost stories. Mary-Ellen was afraid to go out of the house in the evening after hearing about the banshees and the ghosts and the black dogs that everyone had met, and when she had to run down to the closet at the end of the little garden at the back of the house, called the rampar, she ran quickly with her eyes closed.

There was no wireless either in Mary-Ellen's house. The only music she ever heard as a child was when,

instead of a crack, there was a ceili; then, the neighbours brought along a melodeon or a mouth organ or a fiddle, and John-Joe, Mary-Ellen's oldest brother, played his accordion and the men sang the old songs, which were laments and comeallyees.

"They were called that because they always started with the words: Come-all-ye-lads and lassies . . ." Mary-Ellen said, and she would start to sing one for me.

When Mary-Ellen was growing up she rarely saw a real car, what we would call a car. There were very few horses since the farms were small and the fields were dug by hand, and the men rowed their boats out on to the lough, for there were no engines.

Whenever my father brought back any food that was different from our usual food, from his visits to other countries or to the city, Mary-Ellen would exclaim about it and examine it suspiciously. When she was a little girl the food had been very simple and she seldom ate meat, but there was usually plenty of fish, particularly eels, because their father earned his living as a fisherman.

Schools were closed for two weeks in October so that the children could help their families with the potato harvest, and potatoes were by far the most important part of their food. Every evening Packy, Mary-Ellen's second oldest brother, would fetch milk in two tin cans from where the Martins' cow was milked at the house a bit farther up the road, where the water-well was too. There was always froth on the milk in one of the cans, milked straight from the cow, and Mary-Ellen's mother skimmed it off for the hens; the buttermilk in the other she used for the flat scones of soda bread, called farls, that she made every day.

With seven children Mary-Ellen's mother needed to bake a lot of bread and to do a huge washing every day.

Every drop of water had to be carried from the farm well (called Maggie's Well) and every griddleful of soda bread was baked on the stove that had to be kept full of wood or coal from morning to night and needed to be riddled free of ashes hourly.

All the children worked hard in the house, in the tiny garden, on the lough, and especially at the harvest and potato-picking times on the neighbouring farms. The hens lived in a pen in the rampar behind the house but none of Mary-Ellen's family ate their eggs. They were sold so that Mary-Ellen's mother could get money for the children's shoes for wearing on Sundays.

The kitchen where everyone ate and spent their working hours when they weren't out of doors, or at school, was small and dark and warm, with red tiles on the floor. There was an iron stove, with a pipe for the smoke, curving into the wall, with a rack above for clothes, and above that again a shelf with a deckled brass edging, and the ornaments on that only came down to be washed or dusted once a year.

Though I had never seen Mary-Ellen's house I felt I knew it better than my own; and everything on that shelf I knew by heart, for I had made Mary-Ellen recite so often how she helped her mother to take the ornaments down, holding them carefully and holding her breath: two brown china alsatian dogs that her father had won at a fair; two vases with fluted white frilly edges and flowers painted on; a clock with a humpy back; and two willow-pattern plates that an old man called Forbie had given them. We had willow-pattern plates too and I was very pleased about that.

The stove was used for heating the house as well as for cooking and early every morning Mary-Ellen's mother got up first, riddled out the old dead ashes, and lit a new

21

fire. One of Mary-Ellen's jobs was to carry in coal and to collect sticks for kindling. She put these under the stove to dry where their dog often lay.

There was a big wooden settle near to the stove where the children sat, and a big chair on the other side which was kept for their father. There was a dresser with drawers and shelves and on its lowest shelf were the soda farls baked that day and next to it the two buckets covered with wooden lids with all the water for the house, brought up by John-Joe or Packy who carried them on a yoke slung over the shoulders.

By the window was a scrubbed table where the family ate but it was too small for them all to sit at all at once and so the younger children took their food over to the settle by the fire and ate it there.

Mary-Ellen remembered being very hungry in the winter when the lough was too rough to go fishing. "We lived as best we could on the potatoes we stored in pits in the autumn, and any cabbage and leeks we had in our own wee garden." Winter or summer, though, the older children had to help to gather bait for fishing lines, and Mary-Ellen used to feel sorry for her sisters some mornings when their mother roused them for school and they were still tired from the night before when they had stumbled through the damp darkness with only a hand-made lantern (a candle in a jam-jar tied up with string) to guide them as they gathered worms for bait.

Their clothes were hand-me-downs from each other and other people, and although their mother knitted as much as she could, she had little time for sewing or knitting. Mary-Ellen and her sisters knitted all the socks for themselves and their father and brothers, and did the darning. There was no money for games or toys, and the children made their own pastimes and the only bought toys that Mary-Ellen remembered, until the day the parcel came, was a football that the boys had saved for, and the bouncing balls the girls played with at school. All else was carved or whittled. Mary-Ellen had a wooden cat made by John-Joe. He'd carved a round head and a body and arms, all from one piece of wood, and her biggest sister Kathleen had knitted a cover for the cat's dark, hard body.

Behind her back the family called her cat the Tackle, which was what her father called anything or anybody that got in his way, or that he wanted to scold or to make fun of. He didn't like the dog being in the house and if he spied it under the stove he'd shout, "Come out of there, you tackle, and bad cess to you," or if Mary-Ellen had left her cat on the table or on his chair he would say, "Get that tackle out of my sight."

Mary-Ellen wanted to call her cat Bernadette after the saint but her mother said it wouldn't be right. The wooden cat was the only toy she had so she carried it with her where and when she could.

One day the postman came to the door of the house with a parcel addressed to The Martin Family. Mary-Ellen said she'd never forget it to her dying day, how the postman came in and put the parcel on the table over by the window. The postman rarely called at their house. Sometimes he came in, with what he called a letter-with-a-window, which was an official letter, about her father's fishing licence, or at Christmas he delivered a few treasured cards from relatives in America or England. But this time he brought in a big parcel, covered with stamps.

Mary-Ellen and her mother stood and stared at it for a long time after the postman had gone. They turned it round and on one side was the name and address of the

sender – Mrs Chandler, Fort Ticonderoga, N.Y., U.S.A.

"Mrs Chandler," said Mary-Ellen's mother, "is our May-Ellie, my eldest sister." She had emigrated to the United States years before, long before Mary-Ellen was born, while her mother was still a little girl herself. They hadn't heard from her in years, not even a card at Christmas.

"Are you for opening it?" Mary-Ellen asked her mother. Her father was on the lough and her brothers were out at school and so were her sisters. Mary-Ellen told me that she was as afraid that her mother would say yes as she was that she would say no. Whichever she did was going to make Mary-Ellen feel nervous and desperate, either with excitement or with waiting. Her mother said wait, wait till the father got home. Mary-Ellen waited in the garden, near the gate, watching for him, hoping that he'd get home before school home-coming time, so that she could see into the parcel before her sisters and brothers were there to take what she wanted, as they always did, because they were bigger and older.

But they came down the road first and she ran towards them, shouting, so that they began to run towards her, frightened by her voice, alarmed at what might have happened, and when they could make it out, they rushed into the house and crowded around the table, looking at the parcel. But until their father came in they couldn't open it. Their mother tried to get them to lay the table, or to help her redd up the kitchen, but though they did try to help, their hearts weren't in it. They kept looking out of the door for their father.

When at last they saw him coming up from the lough, they didn't run towards him shouting, for fear it would anger or frighten him. Instead John-Joe went to meet him, to tell him the news and he ran in too and went straight over to the parcel and got out the knife he used to cut and trim the worms and hooks and lines, and parted the string. Their mother saved the stamps, and the string, and the first wrapping of paper inside the box which was an American newspaper. Inside of that was another big box and when that was opened there was white tissue-paper around a man's suit of clothes.

Underneath that, in bundles and packages, was a set of clothes for every child, with labels and names. Mary-Ellen's mother kept saying, as they were lifted out one by one – a red pleated skirt like a kilt for Kathleen, a blue dress with a white collar for Bridget, a blue skirt with pleats and braces for Teresa, and white rabbits embroidered on the waistband, check waistcoats and trousers for the boys – half laughing and half crying, "How is it that our Ellie knows all our ones' names and ages so well? What's come over her sending us all this, and never a word from her these years?"

There was a white woolly coat for Mary-Ellen, that felt somewhat like fur, and each girl had a pair of white ankle-socks with a pattern round the tops. That was the first time Mary-Ellen had ever seen ankle-socks, for all the girls wore black knitted stockings at that time. There was a knitted jacket and blouse and skirt for their mother. Then, when everyone had got their parcels, there at the very bottom of the box was another box with Mary-Ellen's name on it. Her mother lifted it out and gave it to Mary-Ellen without opening it. Mary-Ellen was afraid to open it. Her brothers and sisters were all watching her in a ring, and her mother and father standing behind them, but they said go on, and she went down on her hunkers and opened the box. There was tissue-paper and a card on the top and on it was written 'To one

27

Mary-Ellen from another' and her mother read it out and said, "Our May-Ellie's name was by rights Mary-Ellen the same as you. I called you after her."

Then Mary-Ellen opened the tissue-paper which had light gold stars printed on it. And inside the paper a doll was lying, with golden curly hair and closed eyes with black lashes and a white dress, white socks, black shoes and a necklace round her neck. Mary-Ellen looked at the doll, and sighed.

Her mother said, "Lift it out," and Mary-Ellen put her hands into the paper and lifted the doll out, and as she did so, the doll's eyes opened wide, as blue as blue, said Mary-Ellen. She would never forget it looking back at her. She nearly dropped the doll but still no one spoke. Then Mary-Ellen said, "Is it mine?"

"It is yours," her mother said.

"And can I keep it?" Mary-Ellen said.

Whenever she got to this part of her story, her voice always got higher and smaller, and she would look away blinking, and so would I, trying not to cry for her and me and the doll and the moment and for what I knew she had been feeling. And when her mother said, "You can so, it's yours," and Philomena the sister just older than Mary-Ellen began to cry for wanting it, Mary-Ellen knew it was hers, and everyone began talking.

The girls all wanted to look at the doll, but at the same time they wanted to try on their new clothes. Their mother went into the room to put on the new jacket and skirt and the white blouse with its high neck, and when she came out everyone stared at her and their father put his hand on her shoulder in a way Mary-Ellen had never seen before. And then all the sisters and brothers except Mary-Ellen ran in to put on *their* new clothes, and at the very end, their father went into the room, and put on the new suit, and when he came out, they all clapped him and themselves and their mother.

Mary-Ellen was still kneeling, holding her doll and watching, and laughing, and her mother bent down and told her to let Philomena hold the doll till she changed into her new coat. She didn't want to, in case she never got the doll back.

"Any other time," Mary-Ellen said, "I would have been over the moon about the white coat – but I could only think of the doll and I was out of that room and changed like the Creggan White Hare, to get the doll back from Philomena."

Then their mother said, "There's going to be no tea the night with all this consate and admiring, away into the room and out of your new clothes, the fire will be dead on us."

And so slowly they all changed back into their old clothes and sat down to eat, although Mary-Ellen could hardly eat.

The next morning, when she woke early, the doll was still there. When all the rest of the family had gone to school or work she played with it, and talked to it while her mother cooked and baked. And then her mother got out a bottle of ink and paper, to write to her aunt about the parcel, and she told Mary-Ellen to play outside for a while. Mary-Ellen stayed by the gate hoping somebody would pass so she could show them her new doll, but no one passed by. The Car Road was empty and still, except for one man, some distance down the road, standing on steps, clipping a hedge with shears. Mary-Ellen knew who he was, though she had never spoken to him, being a shy child, but she opened her gate, and went down to him, holding her doll carefully and stood at the front of his steps. He did not stop in his work, nor look at her, so

she called up that she had a new doll, it had come from America with her name on it.

The man stopped clipping the hedge and listened, and then leaned down and said, "Show us the doll," and Mary-Ellen handed it up, smiling. He took it and looked at it for a time, and then came down the steps and put the doll on the top step and took his shears in both hands and cut its head off.

The head fell at Mary-Ellen's feet, its hair still curly, its blue eyes wide open; the body fell on the other side of the steps. Mary-Ellen saw the head and the separate body but her voice had gone, as though it too had been severed. She could not speak. The man climbed up the steps again and began to clip the hedge. After a while Mary-Ellen's mother came to see where she was, and found her, mute, in the ditch, with the two pieces of her doll. Something more than a doll had been broken, Mary-Ellen said with a sigh. She never had another doll in her life.

Strawberry Hearts

Strawberry Hearts

When I was a little girl and Mary-Ellen was looking after me, I used to try to get her to come out with me, to do the things she always said she would do, at nights, when she was putting me to bed. "We'll go out looking for strawberries the morrow," she'd say, or, "We'll go to pick sloes." But the next day she would be too busy.

"Away and give my head peace," she'd say. "Haven't I got enough to do without looking for strawberries?" I would go out of the room looking sad, on purpose, and I knew she would be looking at me leaving, and as often as not a little while later I'd hear her calling me. She'd say, "You have me head turned and I'll never get finished and your father will be after me for what's not done but anyway we'll go." And we'd put on our coats and set out.

I loved going to look for things with her, for she knew where everything was to be found: the best rushes for making crosses for St Brigid's day, which was in February, and we put the crosses in the house to keep it holy the rest of the year; the best wild strawberries; and the best places for birds' nests. She knew which trees were fairy trees and to be avoided, but best of all, as soon as we started walking to wherever we were going, there was the chance that she would tell me a story.

One of the places for finding birds' nests was up the old path called Creany's Lane, which wasn't used much, because the last of the Creanys had died and his old house had crumbled into ruin. The banks along the lane were covered in bushes and small trees, elder and willow and ash, hawthorn and blackthorn, all making good cover for birds and their nests. And underneath these trees and bushes grew thick grasses, wild flowers and best of all, wild strawberries in the summer. They grew low down in the shade under the hawthorn and elder and may bushes. You had to kneel down and part the grasses to find them.

One hot day I begged Mary-Ellen to come with me to look for strawberries, and at last, after some grumbling, she and I went up Creany's Lane and knelt down on our hunkers and began to look for the small fruit.

"This loanin is so like the old Inver loanin at home where Jemmy the Bridge lived," Mary-Ellen said, "that you would think you were in it, and that Gusty Cassidy was going to come up over the hill and climb up the pig tree. Only there's no pig tree; and Gusty's dead God rest him, for all the devil was in him as big as a goat."

I knew she was starting a story. I said, "Who was Gusty? And what was the pig tree?"

"Gusty was the biggest boy of the Cassidys, a family who lived a fair bit away from us beyond the Claggan. There were six of them and seven of us, and all my brothers and sisters played with them and walked to

38

school with them. But I being the youngest and at home was more on my own.

"The Cassidys were good enough people but Gusty was a bad boy, with a sly way with him. He used to tease me, and I was frightened of him and well I might be. Only I would never cry, for that was what he wanted. And he would never tease me if John-Joe or Packy was near.

"One of the worst things Gusty did was when he went to find birds' nests. The rest of us would never handle the eggs, or as much as touch the nests, for then the bird would abandon the nest. But Gusty, when he found a nest, stole the eggs, or if they were hatched, would kill the wee scaldies. That's what we called the fledglings. You always knew when Gusty had been bird-nesting by the trail of broken shells or wee dead birds. He'd strangle them.

"One summer's day I went out to find wild strawberries up the Inver loanin, and to get to it you had to walk past Maggie's Well where we got our water from. You never taste water like that now. A woman had tried to drown herself in that well, wonst. I used to wonder why, when the lough, and it full of water, was only yards away. Every time I passed it I wondered what I would have done if I had come on her, lying face down in the water, her legs sticking out, and I used to wonder too if her shoes had stayed on, and how her hair had floated, and would frighten the life out of myself.

"Well, as I was walking down past the well, who did I see but my father on a bicycle. Now he never had a bicycle, but the man who worked as a postman, and lived down the road, had one and he let my father have it for odd errands, if my father gave him eels in return. The bicycle had a carrier on the back where you could sit, and if there was anything I loved, it was to get a spin behind my father on this bike. He stopped and said, 'Are you coming over to the Brine's Joe's with me?'

"Now the Brine's Joe's had a little shop, over by the chapel and the priest's house beyond Biddy's Brae and the Claggan, oh, a good mile away and I loved to go there. But this day, some notion I took, I just wanted the strawberries and so I said no, I would go on up the Inver loanin. My father cycled on and I watched him, wishing in a way I had gone with him. But when I got up the loanin and began to look I was glad I had stayed. The strawberries were so ripe and they were ready to drop.

"Now everyone in our family all picked strawberries in a different way. Some put them straight, one by one, into their mouths as they found them. Kathleen would always save a few to make a mouthful. I always hoarded them up. I thought if you kept them all till the end in a big rich mouthful, you felt the taste in your mind and memory as well as your mouth.

"The way I kept the strawberries as I found them was to thread them on to a sharp piece of grass pulled from its outer sheath, so that they were like a string of beads; red and yellow and stippled where they weren't all ripe. I loved these sharp ones, they added to the taste of the ripe ones.

"I didn't taste even the one as I gathered them, but threaded them on to the stalk, taking care I didn't puncture them too roughly to make them bleed, or break, or fall to one side. Every time I added a strawberry I laid the stalk on the grass, and went on searching. And as I threaded the last one on, well pleased with myself, and my mouth watering, I saw a shadow over me, like a hawk over a sparrow. When I looked up, Gusty was

standing over me. I can see him still, as if he was there in front of me, as sure as God I can.

"'That's a quare lock of strawberries you've got there,' he said, oh I mind it so well, and I didn't say anything but held the stalk tighter. He reached out, and took the stalk, gently enough, from my hand, and then leaned his head back and put the stalk as far as it would go, into his mouth. He slowly closed his lips and pulled the stalk out and it was empty, except for four strawberries up at the end, near the seed, beyond his mouth's reach.

"I knew the feel of the strawberries in his mouth, their red wetness. And as I watched him, I saw my father creeping, like a stoat at a rabbit, up behind him. Gusty looked at me, and then at the last four strawberries and then back at me and he began to laugh. And as he saw that I was not looking at him, but behind him, he turned round, fast as fast, and spun into my father, standing behind and above him.

"'I never ate them,' Gusty said.

"'You never ate what, Gusty?' I can hear my father saying it still. 'Sure I never said you'd eaten anything.' He and Gusty stared at the stalk in his hand, almost empty now, except for the four left, up at one end, and reddened from the blood of the strawberries.

"'What didn't you eat,' he said again, quietly and then suddenly put out his hands and lifted Gusty up by the back of his coat and began to run, quietly, silently, carrying Gusty, as a cat might carry a kitten. I ran behind, and all I could seem to see were Gusty's feet bumping loosely along the loanin. I was shocked by everything that had happened but most of all I think by my father and the way he carried Gusty down the lane to the bicycle, for Gusty was after all a big boy then.

"He got on the bicycle and put me on the carrier and

drove Gusty in front of him until we came to their house. Paddy, Gusty's father, and his mother Maisie were at their tea over by the table and they looked up startled as we came into the kitchen. Paddy sat with his spoon in his tea, transfixed in the middle of stirring it. He had never seen my father in his house before.

"'Tell him why you're here, Gusty,' my father said.

"I wanted to run away, or to run up to Gusty, or to my father, and to say it's all right, I don't care about the strawberries, only leave him alone and let us leave this house.

"'A big man but a wee coat fits you,' his father said, aiming a blow at Gusty's ear. 'Taking the child's strawberries. Sure you'd give anybody the scunder, you bad big tackle.'

"'Don't hit him,' my father said. 'If I'd wanted him to be hit I'd have hit him myself. No. I wanted to ask you if you could spare him for a couple of hours for I have an errand for him to do. I want him to go back up the Inver loanin, or to any place he wants to, and to fill up a stalk of grass this length,' and he held up my empty stalk of sedge, 'and fill it up just the same as it was before, with the same amount of strawberries and of the same ripeness.'

"I felt sorry for Gusty for all I feared him, for I knew that in my long search I had taken nearly all the ripe strawberries. And after he had set off, we left the Cassidys' house, with farls that Mrs Cassidy gave us. I told my father I was sorry for Gusty and he said, 'If it takes him to Doomsday to gather them, if he has to wait till they grow, he'll still fill that stalk. And I'll warrant that he'll not do what he did a second time, after it, the skitter. He's been asking for a tanning for a long time.'

"He put me on the carrier of the bicycle and we cycled

home. And when that evening Gusty came to the house and gave me the stalk full of strawberries, I didn't know where to look.

"It's over thirty years ago," Mary-Ellen said, "but I can see him still holding that string of strawberries, his face as red as the ripest of them. I couldn't have eaten one if you had paid me a fortune." She sat back on her hunkers and began to thread a handful of strawberries on to her grass-stalk.

"But I'll tell you something for nothing now," she said. "You wouldn't have to pay me the day, oh no. I'll have no trouble eating them now."

I was eating my strawberries one by one and thinking about the beginning of her story and something I had to ask. "And what was the pig tree?" I asked. "That was up the loanin."

"Ah, that's another story," she said, "for another time. Now you come over here and see if you can eat these the way Gusty did." And I did, and I could, and I left four on the stalk at the seedy end for Mary-Ellen and we laughed as we went home.

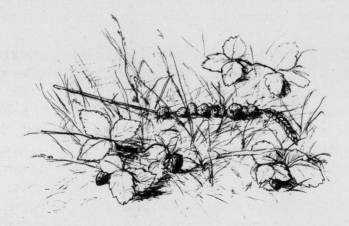

The Pig Tree

The Pig Tree

When I was a little girl, we often had cabbage and bacon for dinner, which was the meal we had in the middle of the day. Mary-Ellen always made the dinner, and she would stand at the door and shout for Tamsie, who worked on the farm my father owned, to come in from wherever he was working, depending on the seasons.

In the spring I'd watch for him coming from the fields, sometimes with a kind of tank fastened on his back, with a thin pipe coming out of it. He sprayed the white potato flowers with the mixture in the tank, and afterwards the fields were a strange glistening blue. Sometimes he'd let me press the little handle, and pump it up and down, and the blue liquid would spray out and pattern the grass around my feet. "Blue stone and soda," he'd say. "There'll be no blight the year."

In the summer he'd come up from the meadows, and in the autumn he'd be in the haggart down by the hay-shed with our two big horses, unloading the haylifter.

In the winter he'd either be in the barns or the byres, or working along the hedges slashing at their branches with a billhook. I would want to watch him doing this, for fear that he would chop away too many branches, and then the birds would have nowhere to build their nests in the spring.

"You'll be foundered out there standing like Paddy's goat," Mary-Ellen would say, and she'd wrap another scarf around my neck, so that my chin was stuck up in the air, and off I'd run to watch for exposed nests and to count how many I had missed.

Tamsie knew how old every bush and tree was in the hedge, and he cut each one in a certain way. If he came on a wren's nest – a round green ball, with a tiny hole in the middle, and if you put your finger inside it was warm and smooth and fine – I would take it home for my room and even Mary-Ellen wouldn't make me throw it out, though she often made me get rid of things I liked that I'd found outside. "I never saw as much rubbidge in my life," she'd say, looking at my shelves with their coloured stones from the lough and feathers and fossils and she'd make a pounce on them, till I stopped her.

Looking at the wren's nest so perfect, so warm, I would wonder why the wrens wouldn't use it a second time. "The swallows always came back to their old nests Mary-Ellen," I said, "so why not the wrens?"

"Because childer like you takes them home," she said. "Ate up your dinner."

The hedgerows, I learnt, grew better for their chopping, and the birds built new nests. When Tamsie came in he would roll up his shirtsleeves to wash his hands in the old yellow sink in the scullery. He called the sink the jar-box, and whenever he rolled up his sleeves, I would see his white, soft, skin, above the mark where the weather had coloured and hardened the rest of his arms and his face. I felt shy at seeing such soft skin on Tamsie.

There were always potatoes for dinner, sometimes boiled in their jackets, which burst in cooking, or peeled and mashed up and speckled green with chopped scallions, and runny with the butter Mary-Ellen made herself in the big wooden churn. This was called champ, and Tamsie and I loved it.

Mary-Ellen often fried bacon for us, or boiled a big ham, but she would never eat these. "It's perties and point for me the day," she'd say. "I couldn't eat that if you paid me." I often wondered why she would never eat bacon or ham but she'd only say, "I took a scunder against it when I was a little girl."

A scunder meant you couldn't eat something without feeling very sick and I knew something must have happened to Mary-Ellen for her to hate bacon so much.

"Why *do* you hate it so much?" I said again one day. Mary-Ellen leaned her chair back from the table on to its back legs and I knew I was going to get a story, and Tamsie was listening too, and we let our dinners get cold while we heard how Mary-Ellen had got the scunder.

When Mary-Ellen was a little girl there was a tree in the Inver lane, near her house, and there was an iron spike stuck deep into the trunk, high in the tree, below the top branches. It was too high up for Mary-Ellen to reach it but her bigger brothers John-Joe and Packy could scramble up by the knots in the bark to swing from the spike, their feet in their big steel tipped boots dangling at Mary-Ellen's eyes.

The tree was called 'the pig tree' but Mary-Ellen had never seen a pig near it.

Mary-Ellen's father's father had kept a pig, and her father always wanted to keep one, but he never could get

the money together. Then when Mary-Ellen was little there was one season when the fishing was great on the lough, so much so that her mother and father went into Cookstown market and bought a pig. It was pink and black when they got it home, and it snorted and squealed as Mary-Ellen's father pulled it out of the carter's crate in the bottom of the cart. Mary-Ellen's father tied a rope round its neck, and pulled it to the small house, where the ducks had always been kept, and put it in there; and that week Mary-Ellen's father and brothers built a low wall with a little gate around the house, so the pig could be outside without wandering. And the house was called the pig craw after that and Mary-Ellen used to go and stand on the low rung of the gate and watch the pig.

It was small when they got it and every day Mary-Ellen's mother saved the potato-peelings and any food there was over and boiled it up for the pig. She added pig-meal and called it a scowder. In the evenings John-Joe used to bring the hot scowder down in a bucket and as soon as the pig heard the noise of the bucket it began moving and grunting with excitement, and almost knocked John-Joe over when he was emptying it out. Sometimes when the pig was eating he'd scratch its back and it wouldn't even move and after a time Mary-Ellen went in and scratched its back too – and felt it was smooth yet bristly.

Mary-Ellen hated the pig. The way it rootled around in the sty, and looked at her with small pale eyes. But she went down to see it every day, and sometimes she would take her piece of bread from tea and hide it in her pocket and throw it to the pig and watch it eat it. The pig got fatter and fatter, but all the same it was never very fat, it always was more long than fat.

"That's the class of pig it is," John-Joe said. The more

Mary-Ellen brought her bread to the pig, the more she began to be able to like it; and soon she felt it was waiting for her, in the evenings, after tea.

"Don't be petting that pig," her father said to her once, "for Jemmy the Bridge will be here afore long."

Jemmy the Bridge was an old man who lived near the round bridge that went over the little river that flowed into the lough. The river was called the Inver.

I knew about the Inver and the loanin beside it where the strawberries grew but I didn't say. Mary-Ellen hated interruptions.

One day when Mary-Ellen came home from school the kitchen stove was covered with steaming pots and pans of water. Even the bath that the family washed their feet and legs in was being used; and the kitchen was full of steam.

Mary-Ellen's father and John-Joe and Packy were there too and Jemmy the Bridge who was sharpening his knife on a greystone. Mary-Ellen was afraid to go closer; the rasping sound hurt her ears.

"That's the best oil-stone in this country," Jemmy said, running his finger along the long knife, "and this knife has stuck a quare lock of pigs. The knife has to be that sharp," he said to Mary-Ellen, "to get through to the heart straight off."

Mary-Ellen ran out of the house down to the rampar, to see if the pig was all right. It stood in a corner of the craw, and as she climbed on to the gate it came over towards her for the bread and as she looked down at it, and it up at her, she heard the men coming down the rampar, and at the same time she heard her mother calling her; but she pretended she didn't hear. Her father said, as he reached her, "Go on up to the house, Mary-Ellen, your mother's looking for you," but although

Mary-Ellen went as if to go, she didn't. She only crept round the corner of the wall, and peeped over.

The men went into the craw and the pig began to squeal even before they caught it. It backed away, but her father caught it by the ears, and tried to wrestle it over, but it tore free and ran between his legs knocking him over.

"Bad cess to you, you tackle," he said, getting up out of the straw, and Jemmy the Bridge caught it by the tail. The pig had been squealing the whole time but now its squeals became like screams, and higher.

Mary-Ellen had never heard a noise like that. It hurt her head and tore the air, and Jemmy pulled the pig between his knees.

Mary-Ellen stared at its front legs and feet, small, straining, its toes scrabbling as it tried to pull away. As she watched its legs, more thin and delicate than she had realised, those dainty legs bent and buckled but the pig didn't fall. Jemmy turned it on its back, and kneeling over it, he cut three little slanty red lines in the pig's throat, like the margin lines in her sisters' school books. Then he pushed the knife further in and pulled it slowly down the pink stomach, and blood followed the line of the knife.

"You have it stuck," Mary-Ellen's father said to Jemmy, but the pig was still jerking and struggling so much that Jemmy fell off, and it got to its feet and staggered to the wall, to where Mary-Ellen was looking over. Its eyes looked as though milk had been poured over them and then Jemmy and her father turned it over again and this time it fell more quietly, only grunting, and as the knife moved along the stomach, the flesh parted and Mary-Ellen could see the pig's inside. It was moving and beating. There were red and white strings tumbled,

and a round thing like a balloon. Jemmy reached in and pulled out the strings. His arms were red to the elbows. The pig stopped jerking and lay still, its eyes open wide, and Mary-Ellen could look no more. She ran up to her mother, who was making soda bread in the kitchen, and she sat down on the settle beside the range and watched her mother pat the soda farls into place on the hot griddle, and blow on her fingers to cool them.

She didn't say anything to her mother about the pig. She didn't say anything at all, but her mother stopped patting the bread and looked at her and lifted her off the settle and carried her into the room and put her on the bed and put a shawl over her and stroked her head and at last Mary-Ellen went to sleep.

When she woke up it was quiet in the house. She went into the kitchen and her mother gave her a slice of farl, and later she went out to see where her brothers were. They were throwing and catching a new white ball which floated when they kicked it. It floated over to Mary-Ellen, and she jumped up and caught it, and saw that it was a balloon. It had a funny milky look like the cover that had come over the pig's eyes.

"Where did you get the balloon?" Mary-Ellen asked.

"That's no balloon, that's the pig's bladder," John-Joe said. "Kick it on over." Mary-Ellen threw the ball over to them.

"Thon pig could have talked to you," Packy said, "you had him that much of a pet," but Mary-Ellen did not answer.

She ran down the road to the Inver and to the pig-tree. The pig was hanging upside down from the iron spike, its stomach open and neat and empty. Its front legs hung nearly down to the ground, and it swung and turned in the evening air.

"I knew then right enough why it was called the pig-tree," Mary-Ellen said. "And after that day I could never eat bacon again in my life."

"You have left the child the same," Tamsie said looking at me; and indeed it was true that after that Mary-Ellen and I always had champ on bacon days, and I never ate bacon again.

The Mad Horse

The Mad Horse

One evening I came home from school late and frightened and Mary-Ellen was at the gate waiting for me. It was bitterly cold, but she had no coat on, and I knew she had been running in and out of the house to look first for me, and then at the clock, to keep herself in a panic. The minute she saw me running up Biddy's Brae she began to run towards me.

"I'm foundered waiting here," she shouted. "I have very little to do, to be out here, catching my death only waiting for you. What time is this to be home or what kept you dallying?"

All the time she was shouting she was running to me, and me to her, and when we met, I buried my face in her overall, and tried to tell her of my terror, when as I walked home a loose horse, all by itself, had come galloping straight at me, up the hill, its eyes wild and rolling, its tail and mane flowing, its hooves clattering like iron on the road.

I had jumped the ditch and lain down behind the hedge, and as the horse galloped by, its hooves ringing out on the road, the noise had suddenly, terrifyingly, stopped so that the silence seemed to press down on my head. I was afraid to move, to raise my face, in case the grass rustled and my eyes would see his, and his great head looming. I thought if he saw me he would jump on me and pulverise me with those ringing iron hooves.

I had never seen a horse like that before. The only horses I knew were our carthorses, Nellie and Teasie, the Clydesdale mares, who worked on our farm. They had shaggy feet, as big as boulders, and they clopped along so slowly, so deliberately, hardly ever changing rhythm, their rumps so much more like moving mounds of earth than flesh, that there seemed no chance of their being able to move themselves into a slow trot, never mind into a gallop. They were more like creatures made from the earth than animals.

Whenever they were in the rampar or yard, waiting between the shafts of a haylifter or cart, occasionally lifting one enormous foot and stamping it down so that the earth around shivered slightly, and blowing out air through their nostrils, I would wonder, as I crept up to them and stroked their noses, at how docile these great animals were, so much bigger than Tamsie to whom they were so obedient. He talked to them as he put the harness on, and shouted and clicked his tongue, and I wondered at how submissive they were to his whistles and instructions of 'whoa' and 'turn', and how stately in their obedience.

They wore greaths, big padded collars around their necks, and their harness and reins and braces were intricately connected together by steel and brass rings, and a big steel bit clanked in their mouths. The greath and

66

harness prevented them from lowering their heads to the grass at their feet, and I would pluck tufts of it and bring it to their mouths and as they munched it bright green juice would trickle down along the sides of their mouths, and I could hear the sound of the bit as it clanked and rattled inside their mouths against their teeth.

The horse that had galloped up the hill seemed hardly of the same species. He had been lean, black, wild, with long angry legs and a narrow head; and his eyes, even at a distance, had not been at all like those large tranquil ones.

"Bad cess to Tommy Riley and his stallions," Mary-Ellen said as she rubbed my hands and then got me my tea. "And if he has to have stallions he should see they are well stabled and not let them get out to go looking after mares, scaring the children." She put my tea on the table in front of me and sat down and tipped her chair back in the way she sometimes did when she intended to tell me a story. I kept very quiet so as not to interrupt its starting.

"I mind when I was wee," she started, "I was always frightened of horses. There weren't many in our part of the country at all at all, for what farms there were, were too small to need horses, and you couldn't keep a horse in hay. So the only time we saw a horse was between the shafts of a cart or trap, to bring the eels to Cookstown, or when a pedlar came around to sell things, like the draper, Willie Jeffers, God rest his soul, who came about once a month. That was always a great occasion. There were drawers in the back of his cart, full of lovely things I thought, and he would pull them out to tempt us: silk blouses or stockings, or petticoats with a frill.

"'Away on with you,' my mother used to say. 'Sure we have no call for that and if we had, we'd have to do without anyway. You'll have the tally-man after us.'

"But then, when I was a bit bigger, a grand new

novelty came into the district, and that was paraffin oil lamps. There was a tin base that you filled with paraffin, and a wick, and the end of the wick lay in the paraffin at the bottom and when you lit the wick, and put a glass globe over it, the flame would burn all night as long as you wanted, steady as a rock. It made a great difference to houses in the evening, and I mind, when I looked out how I could see the windows of the houses that had paraffin lamps in them, shining in the dark, whereas you never could see the houses with candles, only a kind of glow.

"We didn't get a paraffin lamp for a long time after the other houses had them, but I used to watch and wait for the paraffin man to come round the district with his horse and trap, and I would follow him when he was on our road stopping at the houses. He had a big tank in the back of the trap, with a tap on it, and he put a funnel into whatever vessel you'd brought and filled it up. I loved the smell of paraffin, it was something like petrol, and I loved to look at the way the colours of the rainbow mingled in the stains that the drips left on a wet road.

"The man who drove the paraffin trap was called Mickel Heron, and he was what we all called 'away in the head', meaning not exactly right in the head; not mad, but odd, or strange. Wonst, when he was still only a cub, he had to be put away in Omagh for a while. It was as if he couldn't see you, as he drove his trap past you and you only a yard away. He'd never salute you, only would whistle, or sing very loud, looking straight ahead.

"Omagh was where the lunatic asylum was, and I mind that if children then were making too much of a noise, or fighting or whatsoever, their mother would say, 'You'll have me in Omagh afore long, if you don't quet vexing each other and making noise.'

"He seemed harmless enough, although I was scared of him and I was always in the megrims of fear over his horse, for it never looked at you at all when it was coming to pass you, but only when it got fornenst you it would turn its head and look straight at you in a way that put the heart across me. Of course its blinkers made it do that but I didn't know that, I thought the horse was away in the head as well. But for all that, whenever I heard Mickel and his tank coming down the road, I would run after it to watch the paraffin come glittering out of the tap and to smell it, and to look for the colours of its spill on the road."

Mary-Ellen tilted her chair back on to its four legs and stood up and took my plate away, and I was afraid she would stop the story, she was so sad. But she came back in from the scullery with a biscuit wrapped in shiny paper that she had saved for me for a treat.

"I mind so well the song Mickel always used to sing," she said. "It was called *She Moved Through the Fair*, it was always sung in our house, at the ceilis, and it was a sad enough lament, but he'd only sing the same verse over and over again, the one that ended 'As the swan in the evening moves over to the lake.' It would have put your own head round to listen to that for long, and I didn't wonder his own head was turned. But people said he was the best singer in the country, or could have been.

"One day when I was walking by myself down the Claggan, on some errand of my own, to get frogspawn from the flaxhole, or to look into Forbie's house, all on my lone, just like you were the day, I heard this noise. You never heard such a noise, it put the heart out of me – a high voice singing at such a pitch I thought it unearthly, belonging to a banshee or something, and the hooves of a horse hammering and clammering, and the iron wheels

70

of a cart going like the clappers, and then at the latter end, a horse whinnying and crying.

"I pressed myself against the hedge, not knowing where to turn for comfort or escape. Coming over the hill was Mickel, with his horse and trap, only he was standing up, in the trap, with his legs braced against the front board, and whipping the horse on, lashing it he was and I've never seen nor heard a horse go so quickly, before nor since.

"The horse was tossing its head from side to side as it ran, and the cart was tilting from side to side so that the paraffin in the tank was splashing, and the tap was full on so that there was a stream of paraffin behind them. I got a quare scunder of the smell of paraffin that day, I can tell you.

"Mickel stood, keenying and lashing on the horse. He had the funnel stuck on his head, like a crown upside-down, and the oil from it trickling down over his face. But what frightened me most of all was the singing, if you could call it singing, the way he was crying out the last two lines of the song *She Moved Through the Fair*: 'It will not be long love, till our wedding day . . .'

"I stood there as if I was rooted, but as they came nearer, I was able to move and I jumped over that ditch like the Creggan White Hare, much like you did the sevening. Only there was a hedge behind my ditch, a thick thorn one, and God knows how I got through that thickness of thorn. But I did, and as I stood on the other side, by the hole I had made as I forced myself through, all the sound stopped the way it did with you. The hooves, the wheels, the whip, the clammering, the singing and the whinnying. There was nothing else but silence. I was stiff. I didn't dare to raise my eyes to look up for fear of what I would see – the big mad eyes of the

horse looking at me, or Mickel looking at me through the leaves and dripping oil from under the funnel; or both.

"So I waited, with my eyes looking down at my feet, and I can see the shoes I was wearing now as plain as day. A pair that Phelim Grainne had made for Kathleen years before, and that shaped the feet of all of us. And then Mickel began to sing, very softly, like a crooner you might hear on the wireless now. It was the last verse of *She Moved Through the Fair*, and how well I knew it.

" 'Last night she came to me, My dead love came in,' he sang and I never moved, till he had sung the verse through, and when he had finished I raised my head and looked at him, and he was looking at me, his face as wet from the oil as mine was wet from tears. And then he sat down in the trap and the horse moved on, quietly, as peaceably as though it had never run in its life.

"I was still rooted in the field, foundered, when two men came along and they took me back home to my mother. Later, strangers came for Mickel and he was put away again in Omagh and he's there still for all I know."

Mary-Ellen got up to clear the table.

"But there was two things I learnt fornenst it," she said, and her voice was sad. "One was that Mickel *had* the best voice in the country. I'll never hear that song sung like that again. And the other was that I never like to be near a horse. But isn't it the odd thing that the same class of a thing happened to you this very day?"

"Your horse was worse than mine," I said to Mary-Ellen. "And mine just ran on very quickly, and you were at the gate waiting for me. Will you sing me *She Moved Through the Fair*?"

"I don't know that I would have the heart to do it," she said. But she did, that night, when she was putting me to

bed, and I thought of Mickel and I thought of my mother
and I thought, too, that I'd never hear the song sung like
that again.

The Willow-pattern Place

The Willow-pattern Place

When I was a little girl and Mary-Ellen was looking after me, I always had my porridge in the morning on a blue and white willow-pattern plate. There was a high shelf in the kitchen, where I used to eat my breakfast, and propped up on this shelf, all the way round, were big plates with the same blue and white pattern, of a bridge, and a little house, and a man with a whip and, above them all, two birds flying.

I knew the story well – Mary-Ellen often told me it – of two young lovers who were forbidden to meet, and who ran away together, and just as the girl's cross father who had followed them to put them in prison had almost reached them, they were changed into two birds who soared away for ever.

I used to eat my porridge in a certain way, so that as I scraped it up I would show myself the story, bit by bit, and I loved it when my last spoonful showed the birds high up in the blue and white sky.

"There used to be a whole set of that china," Mary-Ellen said, "kept in the china cabinet in the hall. But your mother, God rest her, would never have things kept for what we called good, and wasn't she right. 'I don't believe in it,' she would say. 'You might as well enjoy it while you can.' You'd think she had spied her own fortune. But a lot of it got broken, one way or the other. And what you see is what's left of it now."

I loved the china too and I was glad that my mother had used it and not kept it for best.

Mary-Ellen saw I was sad, and she tipped back her chair the way she did when she might tell a story and said, "I mind the very first time I ever saw that willow-pattern on a plate was when I was only a child, and went into Forbie's house, up by the Claggan on the Car Road. It broke Forbie's heart when he lost that china."

I didn't speak.

"The Car Road," she said, "was the old road that went along the lough shore. It started, or ended, whichever way you looked at it, at the Old Cross, near the graveyard. It went over the Inver past the pig tree loanin and Jemmy the Bridge's house and up past the well and Biddy's Brae and the Claggan, away over to Moortown where the schoolteacher lived and the priest, and where Brine's Joe had his shop, and there it joined a bigger road that would have brought you to Cookstown if you'd followed it long enough.

"Now up beyond the Claggan the road turned sharply so you would think it had ended entirely, and near that corner were five or six houses, gable ends on to the road, built around a clearing and just beyond that was a flaxhole. They called that place the Claggan because it means the Village, or so your father says, although I would never have called it a village myself with only that

80

wee lock of houses and no shop, nor chapel nor school."

"What was a flaxhole?" I said quickly, to pretend I hadn't interrupted.

"A flaxhole?" she said surprised. "Oh, a flaxhole was a dam of water dug out at the edge of a pasture. The water had to be stagnant – it couldn't be running water like in a river or a ditch. We always found our frogspawn and tadpoles in the spring in flaxholes. That was the time of the linen industry.

"The water in the flaxhole heated up in the summer and the flax was put in there to soak and rot. The flax was all to be pulled by hand, and a terrible job it was, it would have broken your back, and it was always full of thistles and weeds. Now every stalk of flax had a core that would make the linen, and it had to be crushed and retted. It was crushed by a big round stone wheel, and afterwards the men put the sheaves of flax into the water and held it down with big stones collected from all over the place. You never see flax now, nor a flaxhole, well it's hard enough to see linen itself, but I can always tell where one was from the boulders round about.

"The flax stayed in the water for weeks and it got hot and slimy and it had all to be pulled out of the water by hand again and spread out over the grass and dried and turned, and dried again, before it could go to the scutching mill, where as often as not it all went up in smoke and you lost your crop and all your labour. Ah, it was a tedious old crop, flax, right enough, and it was a hungry greedy crop too, but the fields around the Claggan were good flax fields and there was money in it. I miss it, the look of it, its beautiful blue colour. The fields were the colour of a summer sky, and when it was scutched it was so golden that it burned and glimmered as though the sun and moon had mixed and fallen on it. You never saw such a colour, except maybe *your* hair when you were only a wee child."

That was the first time I knew the meaning of the word flaxen that I had so often read in fairy stories, but I didn't say that to Mary-Ellen.

"The other thing you do forget," she said, "was the smell of rotting flax that hung all over the countryside at that time. It was a smell that got everywhere, so strong and sour, but after a while you didn't notice it at all, at all.

"Anyway, the flax pullers lived in these cottages, in the Claggan, only by that time they were all getting old. Some of them had never married, the two old Curran brothers now, John-Joe and Ned, they'd never married, and they lived in one of the end houses next to Forbie, and next door to that there was Gulliver and his two sisters; and beside them were the Croziers – they were twins, the only twins in the district, and they had married sisters; but both of them had died, and their children over the water. Martha Coyle was in the end house, who said she saw visions and nearly lived in the chapel, she was there that often.

"I never knew a cleaner daintier old man than Forbie. His heart was scalded with Gulliver who persisted in picking his flowers. Gulliver was called that because he was moon-mad and wandered all over the countryside, sometimes so far that the neighbours had to go out to look for him. But he was harmless enough, sure they all were.

"John-Joe Curran was a rhymster – he always spoke in rhymes when he did speak, which wasn't often, and whenever we met him we would try to get him to say something, to hear how he could get the words to match, and his brother Ned never spoke a word.

"One evening when I was coming home from the

graveyard after watching for my father on the lough, I met John-Joe. He was a wee man, and dark, and he always wore a low hat with a brim, there was no other hat like that in the country. You could hardly see his eyes under it.

"He stopped by me, which wasn't like him, and I stopped too and looked up into his face under the hat's shadow, and saw that his face was wet, that tears were running down it, down the two wrinkles that went down his cheeks like furrows in a field.

"He had a moustache, and the tears congregated at the end of this moustache and they dropped, so that I thought to hear them splashing.

"I didn't know what to do or say, I had only seen one man cry before and that was Mickel Heron, the day he lost the head altogether with the oil in the pony and trap. I looked at John-Joe and he put out his hand at me and said, 'Two great men are lately dead. Father Walsh and our Ned,' and went down the road to the Claggan. I ran on, and into my mother and repeated to her what John-Joe had said, and it was true, his brother had died, suddenly, and when John-Joe had run over to Moortown to get the priest, his old housekeeper had met him at the door of the parochial house with the news that the old priest had just died also.

"It had comforted John-Joe greatly, it was said, that his brother should have been called at the same hour with as good a man as the old priest, but when I met him that day and looked up into his countenance I knew the meaning of grief.

"Then in the same year Martha died and Gulliver's two sisters and there was only old Forbie and John-Joe and Gulliver left in the Claggan to fend for themselves and the houses began to slide back into the ground. They were made of stone and mud, thatched and whitewashed, and they were warm and snug but as soon as the thatch began to rot it let in the damp, and soon after that the house just went back into the earth.

"But Forbie kept his house up lovely, and on the shelf around the kitchen he had the very same blue and white china you're eating off now. All arranged the whole way round. Even looking into Forbie's kitchen over his half-door made my heart content, to see the brass and the china and the fire, all glittering.

"In the garden in front he had flowers that I had never seen anywhere else – well, there were no flowers to be seen, the people hadn't time for growing flowers, and what was nearer the mark, they had no land for flowers. You needed any bit of spare ground you had for growing potatoes and vegetables for hungry mouths. But Forbie had a bigger garden and only himself to feed, so he had roses, and I don't know what else; but the best thing he had, and I could never get over it – I would make an excursion to see it every summer, well the whole family did – was a big tall blue flower, like a church spire, you never saw such a blueness with a dark centre, and it was bluer even than the flax. It was called a delphinium, and I could never get over the name and the way it suited the flower.

"Those were hard times in Ireland. There was a Civil War, brother fighting brother, in other parts of the country. It was a terrible tragedy and we would hear of the shootings and the killings. The Troubles they're called now, but we were never too troubled by them, being so far away and being such a poor district. But the fear of God was in us of the Black-and-Tans. They were soldiers of a kind, criminals let out of prison in England, to come over here to subdue the fighting. After they

came over nobody ever tried to frighten us with stories of banshees or black dogs or bogey-men any more. 'The Black-and-Tans will get you' was threat enough for us.

"One day I heard the noise of a big engine coming down the road. You never heard or saw a car in those days, only if you went into Cookstown on market day when you'd see a lorry and a car or two. So when I heard this noise I ran out and there was a big lorry coming slowly down the road with an open back and sitting in two straight lines facing each other were soldiers with guns. After all the threatening I had had, I had almost come not to believe in the Black-and-Tans but here they were, in their tan uniforms with black facings. I went in to my mother like the Creggan White Hare, screaming, and she dropped the farl she was making. She couldn't make out what I was screaming, and she put my head under her apron and rocked me and looked out and saw the lorry and the soldiers as they went on down the road.

"She crossed herself, and when my father came in from the lough they speculated about what the soldiers were doing in such a far-away district, away from the trouble and fighting, and my father said, 'They'll be looking for someone on the run.'

"On the run," Mary-Ellen said, for she could see I was dying to ask, "was when you were wanted by the police and had escaped and were hiding. So. That made me the more frightened, and that evening my mother put a bar across the door. We were sitting around the fire and it nearly bed-time when there was a knocking at the door. 'Whist and don't open it,' my mother whispered, and then we heard Forbie's voice calling, and my brother ran and opened the door and Forbie came in, and when we looked at his face we knew that something terrible had happened.

" 'They have my house ruined,' he said. 'They've not left gubbens of it.' And for the third time I saw a man cry.

" 'Sit down, sit down,' said my mother, 'and take a cup of tea and tell us your story. Who has it ruined?'

" 'I can't sit,' Forbie said. 'I'm away over to get the master or the new priest. I was in the Cookstown the day, the only time I have left home this sixmonth, and I walked there and hardly able to do it, and when I got back home . . .' He stopped, in tears again and got up and went to the door and my mother threw a shawl over her head and my father pulled on his coat and we all followed running one after the other, in the half light, down the Car Road to the Claggan, following Forbie.

"Forbie's door was open, his garden trampled, his roses and bushes lying flat broken, and on the little path leading to the door and by the door and on the upturned soil, and under the walls lay hundreds of bits of blue and white china. They looked almost like growing things in that light. Our father bade us wait at the gate and he and my mother went up the path and into the house, but I followed too. Everything was lying on its side or back and Forbie's buttermilk can was stamped flat and there were more bits of his willow-pattern plates on the floor, and Gulliver was sitting in the middle of it all and John-Joe beside him.

"John-Joe looked up at us, and said slowly and sadly, 'The Black-and-Tans were here the day, and now there's nothing left to say. They shot the plates and wrecked the house, and lucky it is they didn't shoot us.'

"I couldn't get over how he spoke like that so naturally even though he was so sad and so was I and my mother began to cry as she bent to pick up bits of china from the ground. There were only two plates left that weren't broken. My father went with Forbie over to the school-

master's house, and Forbie stayed there that night and the next. In the end he never did go back. He went to live with the schoolmaster's family and I was always very envious of the children, for they had Forbie to tell them stories and he built them a house in a tree in the garden. But he gave *us* the blue and white plates.

"Soon after that, John-Joe Curran died; and Gulliver was put away in Omagh, alongside Mickel for all you know; and the only signs of the Claggan now are the heaps of green earth where the houses used to be, and the white stones lying round what was the flaxhole, and that long blue flower.

"And now," Mary-Ellen said, "are you for finishing that porridge, or are you going to be sitting there all day, puddling?"

"I'm going to be there all day, puddling," I said. And Mary-Ellen laughed.

The Charm and the Pin Tree

The Charm and the Pin Tree

When I was a little girl, I once read a story about a child
who put any tooth that came out of her mouth under her
pillow at night, and when she woke she found a silver
sixpence instead. It was the wintertime when I read the
story and I had both a cough and a loose tooth, and I
pulled at the tooth to get it looser. When Mary-Ellen
pounced on me and told me to give over fiddling at my
mouth and asked me what I was at, I told her I was at
getting money for my tooth.

"And who do you think's going to give it to you,
pray?" she said. And I said, laughing, "The fairies take it
from under your pillow and leave a silver sixpence." I
was laughing because I didn't believe in fairies, and
although she said she didn't, I knew she would never go
near the Fairy Tree in the middle of the Fallow Field, and
that she would let no one ever cut or even break a branch
from it.

But she laughed too. "Isn't it well to be some," she

said. "You're brev and innocent," which meant I was cunning. "The fairy you're thinking of, if I'm not badly mistaken, is me or your father creeping in after you're asleep to put the sixpence under your pillow. Ah well, chance would be a fine thing and pigs might fly, and there's no harm in hoping. But if I had a sixpence for every tooth I've lost I'd have a fortune behind me, though it would only have been thought a consate when I was a child to have put a tooth under a pillow to get money. I never had money when I was small; no child had. The only time I ever saw us children with money was wonst when a visitor gave me sixpence after he had been visiting the Old Cross – and the time Gusty took the luck pennies from the Pin Tree. You always knew a coin from the Pin Tree because it was so bent from having been hammered into the trunk of the tree. We thought Gusty would surely suffer for taking things from the Pin Tree, that it could only bring him bad luck, and maybe it did, for he died early, did Gusty."

I knew who Gusty was, the boy who had eaten Mary-Ellen's strawberries, but I never spoke.

"There was a story told about Gusty and the pennies from the Pin Tree and the Charm," she said, and she looked at me, and I knew I might get the story if I didn't ask her too much, so I just kept quiet; but I couldn't because of my cough.

Mary-Ellen said, "And I wish I could get you the charm for that cough, the way it's hanging on it seems nothing else will shift it and you have my head turned plughering away. If you go to bed early the night with a soothener I'll maybe tell you about the Pin Tree. And the charm. And poor Gusty, God rest him. If you're good."

I was good, or good enough, and when I was in bed Mary-Ellen sat in her chair and tilted it back and started her story, the kind I loved the very best about when she was a little girl.

"If you walked on down past Kitty's house," Mary-Ellen said, "you came to the end of our wee road, and lying just beyond its end, between it and the lough, was the graveyard where I watched for my father on the lough, and in the graveyard was the High Cross. There had been an Abbey there wonst, but the abbey's long gone, nor sight nor sound of it left but the Cross still stands on account of the High Cow."

I knew about the Cross and its mortar being mixed with the milk of the High Cow to give it its lasting powers but I liked her telling me things over and over again.

"Round this Cross, it being a holy place, the people had buried their dead; and it was a lovely graveyard, the nicest you'd ever see. I have only one wish for when I die, and that's that I'll be buried in that graveyard near the lough shore."

I never liked to interrupt Mary-Ellen when she was in the middle of a story in case she stopped and didn't start again but I couldn't help saying, "A *lovely* graveyard?"

"Ah, it wasn't like the ones you see now," she said, "with all their new marble and cement. This was more like the Fallow Field with the odd big stone half buried in it, and flat slabs, where we would lie, pulling the moss that had grown over the names of the people lying beneath. That was how I learnt my alphabet, just spelling out the names of the long-gone dead letter by letter, as I lay there, looking out at the lough shore and waiting to see my father rowing home after the fishing.

"There was a quickthorn hedge round the graveyard, except on the side where the lough shore was the boundary. Just inside the gate there was a big beech tree

95

with low branches, and its trunk and lower branches were covered and studded and stuck, every inch of it, with pins and pennies and coins of all kinds, brooches and clips, and nails, and any odd bits of metal, and most of all with pins; safety pins and sewing pins, any class of pin. It was called the Pin Tree, and everybody believed something different about that tree, depending on what they wanted to believe.

"What was certain was that it *was* a wishing tree. The older people believed it had water-power – the lough water was supposed to have magical qualities, and it's true that water did always lie in a hollow in the tree even on the driest days. Others thought it was a curing tree, that if you left something in it you would get better of your pains. But the belief most people held was that if you put something into the tree you would always come back to fetch it; and that was why metal was always put in, for it lasted the longest. I think, myself, that emigrants started that wish on the tree, years before, in the hope they would come back to where they were leaving."

"Emigrants?" I said but very quietly, for this was the second question, and she hated questions.

"Emigrants were all the people who had to leave their family and their country to be able to live. There was no work at home then, and too many mouths to feed, so people went off to seek work where they might find it. Do you mind thon parcel I got with the doll in it, from Ellie? She was an emigrant, and my mother's sister, and the eldest daughter in the family, and she sent money back to help rear the other children in the family. Ah, emigration was supposed to be the curse of Ireland and certainly it must have broken many a heart. Parents knew they would never see their children again, and the children knew they were leaving for ever. None of my mother's family ever did see Ellie again. She never got back. That's what the songs and laments we sang were all about, separation and heartbreak and starvation.

"Whenever we went down to the graveyard we always went over to the Pin Tree to see what new thing might have been stuck into it. To a stranger it would just look like a jumble, a mix-up of old coins and screws and pins, but we knew the place of everything, and when it had been put there, and often *who* had put it there. After new visitors had departed there would be a penny or even a sixpence half-hammered into it, but we would never touch it.

"And then, one time, we noticed, me and my sister Philomena, and Packy, that there were no coins where coins had been. At first we thought they had maybe fallen out of the tree, and we looked around the bottom and in the roots but we really knew, even while we looked, that there was no way the money could have fallen out: it had all been too well hammered in. And time after time, after that, we would mark that some visitor had left a coin, and we'd mark, too, that the next day it was gone. And we knew without saying that it was Gusty who was taking it.

"We knew, because we knew him of old, and we knew also because he was the kind of boy who couldn't keep anything to himself. Nothing was any good to him unless someone else wanted it, so he had to show off that he had got money before he could get the worth of it. He began to walk around with a hand in his pocket jingling and jangling the coins. And in those days hardly anybody had money to spare for jangling. What money did come into any house went straight out again, on necessities – there was no time for it to be rattling in pockets. And children had no money at all. So you couldn't help but notice Gusty rattling and clinking like a remittance man. You'd wonder he didn't have more wit although he wasn't so soft as to do it in front of grown-ups.

"We wondered at him stealing luck like that, it was a dangerous thing to do, we believed, and I still do. Whoever had left the money behind had left some of their hope there, and hadn't left it for Gusty to thieve. But we never said anything, for we were afeared of Gusty. We listened to him rattling the money, and we waited.

"Now up in the other direction from the graveyard past our house, up the lough shore, was Golloman's Point, and at the very tip, so that you'd think it was floating, there was a white house with so many trees around it that it was very dark and in that house lived Barney Dugh who possessed the charm."

All the time Mary-Ellen was talking I was trying not to cough, but the harder I tried, the more my throat tickled, and I suddenly started to cough as if I was choking. She got up from her chair and got me more of my linctus, and as she gave it to me she said, "I wish to God I could take you to Barney the night to get you shot of this cough.

"The charm," she said, as I lay down again, "was also called the gift, or the cure. It was passed from one person to another over the generations and was a secret that nobody else knew. It was a gift, and whoever possessed it could rid people of certain ailments. It was a most odd thing when you think of it, the cure, and there's many that will doubt that such a thing existed. But it was commonplace in our time and anybody could have told you any number of things that had been cured by the charm.

"Now in those days, you never saw a doctor unless you were dying and then he was no use. Anyway, there were no doctors near – you had to go to Cookstown to get one, and he cost a mint. So if you had a bad back-ache, or a cough like you have now, or a pain in your stomach, or whooping-cough, or warts, you would go for the cure. And there were more ailments like that around then.

"I mind once going with my father, up to Golloman's Point, to visit Barney Dugh, the day he had ricked his back rowing into the lough shore when a sudden storm blew up. He was near crippled with it, and afeared that he'd not be able to go on the lough again at all, and my mother said, 'What would befall us if that should happen? Go you on down to Barney's and get the cure this very day before the crick has settled into your spine.' And I walked with my father, I mind it so well, for I wasn't often out walking with my father. I hadn't started school yet and he took me along for company, or maybe I pestered him to come with him. I had never been into Barney Dugh's house, and I wanted to see what a charmer's house looked like. But once you were in it was the same as anybody else's house. As my father entered – and he had only just hurt his back that very day – Barney got up from the settle by the fire and said, 'You have come about your back.' My father said, 'I have,' and straight away Barney went into the wee room behind the kitchen and stayed in there maybe for five minutes, and as he came out, my father heard his back click, and what's more, so did I, and the pain had gone and that's as true as I'm sitting here telling you the story. My father brought him up a fine catch of eels the next day.

"Well, one day, long after we had found that Gusty was stealing from the Pin Tree, we heard our mother telling our father that Maisie, Gusty's mother, was lamenting because Gusty's hands had suddenly got

99

covered in warts. We never said a thing, Packy, nor Philomena nor me, but as soon as the tea was over and cleared up we were out of the house, and down the road like Creggan White Hares, past Gusty's house, to see if we could see him and the punishment he had brought on his hands. But we didn't see him.

"But the next day at school Packy and Philomena watched and though Gusty tried to keep his hands in his pockets the teacher shouted at him for so doing and he had to take them out for writing. And there, right enough, were warts, big ones, over the back of his hands. Packy and Philomena couldn't but look and Gusty knew full well what they were thinking, that the warts were a judgement on him from the Pin Tree, but nobody said anything. The warts stayed and Maisie, his mother, told our mother that she had tried every remedy, she had rubbed the warts over with a potato and buried the potato, she had made poultices of boiled docken leaves and liniments; but all to no avail.

"'Take him you to Barney Dugh's,' my mother said, 'and get them charmed.' But Maisie said that was only nonsense, to believe in such things was foolery. And when my mother was telling this all to my father, and us listening, quietly over on the settle, she said, 'And sure the charm wouldn't work for her anyway, when she doesn't believe in it.'

"'If she'd heard the way my back felt the charm she wouldn't be so sure it was nonsense,' my father said.

"The warts got worse. Soon after, I saw Maisie coming up the road with Gusty beside her, and ran in to tell my mother.

"'My head's turned with him,' Maisie said, 'and I'm defeated the way he's itching and the look of his hands would give you a scunder. So I'm away over to Barney's to see if he can cure him.' And my mother said that she would go with her, not wishing to miss what might happen, for Barney knew Maisie had never believed in his gift and indeed had spoken against it. And I went too, so as not to be left alone in the house, and thrilled I was.

"When we went into his house Barney got up, just the way that he had when my father had come in, and he said, looking straight at Gusty, 'You have come about your hands,' and his mother said, 'He has,' and Barney went into the room behind the kitchen and when he came out he said, 'I can do nothing for you, you have some other charm on you.'

"And Maisie said, blazing up, 'I never went to another man for a charm and I never will, nor to you again. I'm only here because nothing and nobody else can help us and Gusty is astray in the head with the look and feel and itch of his hands. But I never tried another charm.'

"'Well I can do nothing for you,' Barney said again, looking at Gusty. I can see that look now, but Gusty couldn't look back at him, well Gusty never could, so *that* was nothing strange. 'You will get rid of your ailment,' Barney said, 'when you have got rid of the other charm, whatever that may be.'

"Maisie and my mother and Gusty and me left Barney's house and all the way home Maisie raged about Barney's riddles, and said she could make neither head nor tail of his meaning and questioned Gusty whether he took Barney's meaning and Gusty denied it. But I knew from the way he looked at me and then at the ground that he understood as well as I did. And that evening when Packy and Philomena and I went down to the Cross, there were farthings and half pennies and pennies and threepenny bits all hammered back in, far more than we had ever divined Gusty had taken; and I knew that he had

understood what Barney was saying in the same way that I did."

"And did the warts go?" I said.

"They did," Mary-Ellen said, "and soon after. But Maisie never fathomed what had happened and if you ever talked about Barney and his gift she would say, it's all foolery and superstition, and we never corrected her. What would have been the use? But Gusty never took money from the Pin Tree again: and maybe emigrants did get home, and found their talisman still waiting for them."

She got up from the chair and came over and as she did, the tooth that I had been jiggling about with my tongue came out. There was some blood and a gap in my mouth but I was pleased and Mary-Ellen said, "Put it under your pillow. There's no harm in hoping."

As she stooped over me to tuck me in I whispered, "And if I do get a silver sixpence, I'll keep it to put it into the Pin Tree."

"If the pair of us ever get back," she said, and she smiled.

The Petrified Stone

The Petrified Stone

For a long time after my mother died I was afraid that Mary-Ellen, who had helped to look after me from when I was only a little baby, might go away and leave me. But she never did, even for a night, and when my father was away on business, I would never feel lonely, for Mary-Ellen always left her door open all night.

Her bed was just on the other side of the wall from me and I liked to think of her there, and sometimes I would tap on the wall and she would tap back if it wasn't too late or too early. The wallpaper in my room had a pattern of roses on it but Mary-Ellen's room had pink plaster. Although I was happy that Mary-Ellen never went away from my house, even for a day, I sometimes wondered whether she thought about going back to her house beside the lough shore near to the big Cross, and seeing all her brothers and sisters again. I never asked her in case it put the idea into her head which was what she used to say to me.

"Who put that idea into your head?" she'd say, if I asked her something that surprised her. I wondered if she dreamed of her home at night, on the other side of the wall from me, and thought she must, for after all, didn't I dream of it, even though I had never been there? Mary-Ellen had told me so much about it and the people around about that I felt I knew it better than my own house.

One hot summer's night, when I was lying waiting to go to sleep and finding it very hard because it was still so light outside, and the window was open, and I could hear the noises of the farm outside, and Tamsie whistling, and the hens on the path making low chawking noises in their throats, and further away the sounds of other luckier children, still up, calling to each other, I scratched with my nail at the centre of a rose on my wallpaper, and the pattern came away, so that I saw the bare wall underneath. I scratched on at that and a little bit of white powdery plaster trickled out. After that, every night, I scratched the hole a little bit deeper. I used to wonder what part of Mary-Ellen it would come out at, when I'd finished. She never noticed the little tunnelly hole, even when she was making my bed, it was so much in the centre of the pattern, and I thought when I could see through it I could watch her dream and also watch that she wouldn't go away.

I started making the hole at about the same time that my father was talking to Mary-Ellen about something he didn't want me to hear. I first knew that was so when I went into the room that he called his office, and he was sitting behind his desk and Mary-Ellen was standing in front of it. Instead of taking me on to his knee as he usually did, he stopped talking, and told me to go off on

some errand to fetch something he didn't need, so I knew
that it was only to get me away.

I was very vexed and as soon as Mary-Ellen came out
of the office-room I ran to her and asked what my father
had been saying and she would only say "Little pitchers
have big ears". I began to cry and she cuddled me then
and said it was nothing bad they were talking about, nor
was she being scolded, but it was a surprise that might or
might not happen, and I was not to fret.

After that I pestered her to tell me what it might be,
and I tried to guess but she wouldn't say even if I was
right or wrong. I said I thought it was cruel not to tell me,
when all my thoughts were on what it could be, she only
said, "Do you know what thought did? It stuck a feather
in the ground and thought it would grow a hen . . ." and
I could get nothing more out of her.

But one day my father called me into his office and
took me on his knee and told me that he had to go away
on a long journey and he hoped I wouldn't be too upset;
but that he had planned that Mary-Ellen and myself
would go to stay in her house, with her brother and her
sister-in-law who lived in it now, and her old mother.

I felt then that I couldn't wait till my father would go,
but I saw that although he was glad that I was not going
to be unhappy while he was away, he didn't want me to
be too happy about it. So I wasn't. I *was* sorry he would
be away, and we planned all we would do when he got
back. But all the same I could hardly wait till I could see
all the places in Ardboe I knew so much about.

When the day came for us to leave I was awake early,
and I scratched at the hole but I didn't care any more
about it getting deeper. Mary-Ellen had packed for the
both of us the night before, and when she came in to

rouse me, she was dressed in her Sunday Costume and her stockings, and she had the tight deep waves in the front of her hair that came after she had washed it and put in big steel pincher things all night.

It was a long drive and by the time we got to Cookstown I was tired but excited, for that was where her father had bought the pig. But it was still many miles along roads that got narrower and wilder until Mary-Ellen said, "We're in Ardboe now," and I saw the schoolmaster's house and the chapel and the new Post Office. I made my father slow down as we passed the schoolmaster's house, to see if the house that Forbie had built in the tree was still there, but Mary-Ellen laughed and said it was gone long since and the tree with it, no doubt.

And then we were at the Brae Hill, and there was the Fairy Tree still standing and I could hear in my head Mickel's horse running away. And as we turned the corner at the Claggan there below us was the lough. I could never have believed it was so big. Only some pale blue low hills far away showed where the land began again on the other side.

"That's Lurgan," Mary-Ellen said. "I wonst went there on the boat."

I still couldn't see the High Cross.

"That's the wonder of it," Mary-Ellen said. "It stands on the only eminence along the lough shore and yet you don't see it till you're up against it."

Along the shore I could see trees with the nets hanging shining between them, like enormous spider webs.

"Sally trees they are," Mary-Ellen said, "and many's the time I was sent out to break a switch from them, to be beat with. When they swished it at your legs it made a whistling noise and you'd always try to jump over it but it only caught you the harder coming back."

"That wasn't fair," I said, "to have to pick your own punishment."

"It never did me a hait of harm," she said, "and after all there were seven of us, and each one bolder than the next. My mother's head must have been turned, when I think of the botheration you are, and you only the one." I was glad that Mary-Ellen had never chastised me like that.

"And there's the Inver and here's home," she said in a sudden voice, and we stopped outside a house that wasn't like the house of my dreams at all, but had tiles and no green roof, and a porch with glass windows, and it was bigger. But Mary-Ellen's brother and mother and sister-in-law all came out and began to greet us and exclaim over me, so that I felt shy and I hadn't time to think. And when the noises had stopped I heard the lough, the slap and sough and hiss of water beating on the shore. Mary-Ellen had never told me about that.

We went into the house and there were eels and farls for tea. That was the first time I had ever eaten eels. They were like little slices of white meat and we ate them with our fingers and mopped them up with the soda bread and I kept looking around the kitchen to see what I knew. There was the same stove that the tackle had crept under; and the alsatian dogs were still over the mantel, and the wavy vases, and Forbie's plates.

After tea my father kissed me goodbye, and to cheer me up Mary-Ellen said we could walk to the Cross and Packy her brother came with us. We walked past where Kitty's house had been and there was the graveyard and the Cross high above me with one of its arches and arms broken off. There were iron railings all around it.

"They put them up because emigrants leaving or visitors would take a bit of the Cross as a souvenir," Mary-Ellen said, "and what the rain and wind of a thousand years couldn't do, the depredations of people could."

I thought of the High Cow and her magic milk and we went into the graveyard, to look for the Pin Tree, but it had gone.

"It was killed with the copper-poisoning," Packy said. "I said they should have kept the stump on as a relic but nothing would do but they would chop it down. They're mad keen on tidying now," Packy said. "All has to be edged and trimmed."

The graveyard was still beautiful, but full of all kinds of headstones. Mary-Ellen showed me the old one she had lain on as a child and I pulled at the moss that covered the names and read John Sinnamon Devlin who departed this life 1813 and his wife Eileen R.I.P.

Everywhere there were new noises; the thorn-trees and the yews creaked, the rooks and the gulls shrieked, and behind everything was the big moving noise of the water slapping against the shore, and rocking the little boats that were moored in narrow inlets.

"You never said about the noise," I said to Mary-Ellen and she said, "What noise?" and when I said the lough noise she said she never heard it, she was that accustomed to it and she still didn't hear it, even though she had been away so long.

"Would you like to go out in the boat for a spin?" Packy asked me and I could only nod, and another man came down the path, past the sloe bushes, and they helped me and Mary-Ellen into the boat and Packy rowed out past the stones, and then put the engine on, and away we went. The engine sat all by itself in the

middle of the boat and Packy said he had got it out of an old car. The water was as smooth as silk and when I looked back there was a double wave unfurling behind us and spreading out like a fan. The shore got very far away, and we saw ahead of us a little island, Ram's Island, and Packy said that his father's father had walked to that island over the ice, the year of the Big Winter.

"Do you ever go swimming?" I said to Packy and he laughed and said he had never learnt to swim and never would, and then Francey, the other man in the boat, told Mary-Ellen what his father had said when he had put a bathroom into his house, "I said to him when the bath was all installed and the water all hot and working, would he take a bath. And he started back and said, 'I haven't fished every day on the lough nigh on forty years to be drowned at the latter end in me own front room.'"

Mary-Ellen laughed and laughed and so did I and then she said that no fisherman had ever learnt to swim that she knew of. "The lough claims one victim every year," she said, "one person dies in it every year and it's believed that if you're marked for it, she'll get you whether you can swim or not."

"But the water's so calm," I said. "If you floated you could be rescued."

"Ah but it wouldn't be calm the day she wanted you," Packy said smiling, "and if you can't swim you'll go down all the quicker, and that would be better, for the lough will have you if the mark's on you, should you swim like an eel."

"You'll frighten the child," Mary-Ellen said but I wasn't frightened at all. We turned the boat around in a big circle near some floating bits of cork and Francey made the engine quiet so that we almost stopped and Packy pulled up the line from underneath the cork, and on every hook there were eels, long, black and silver, jerking and flipping, so alive as they died, twisting frantically, looping and coiling trying to get clear of the hook impaled in their throat.

Packy pulled each hook clear and threw the eels into a box full of water beside the engine on the floor of the boat, and they slithered in and out themselves, in a thick tangle.

They only lifted a few eels before they started the engine again and headed for home, and Francey gave me the tiller and I steered.

When we got in, they lifted the box out and Packy showed me how to clean and skin the eels. He dug his fingers in sand, caught one eel tightly, hit its head on a stone and then slit its throat, slicing through flesh and bone without going through the skin at the back of its neck; the almost severed head fell back and Packy put his thumb into the slit and pulled, and the skin peeled away like a banana and the eel's body came out, clean and soft and white. He dropped the skin, and it lay at my feet, a little empty wrapping, and after some tries, when I cut too far and cut the eel's head off, I could do it well enough.

"There's a good girl," Packy said. "Now there's some childer as wouldn't do what you've done. They would turn away, though I think if you can eat something you should know where it came from and how you came by it.

"Did Mary-Ellen ever tell you," he said "about the powers of lough water? That it can petrify." I thought that petrifying meant frightening but he said no, it meant that if you put wood into the water and left it for seven years, when you came back it would have changed into stone.

"Ah, Mary-Ellen here," he said laughing, "had every piece of wood she could lay hands on hid in some nook or cranny all along the shore when she was a child. Only she could never mind where she had left them."

He gave me the handle of an old knife and I hid it in a crack by the water's edge and swore as I stood there that I would one day pick it up, made into stone. Then we walked home, and Packy took the eels into the house.

Mary-Ellen and I walked on up the road towards Golloman's Point, and there lying, among the rushes, was a flat white stone, and in the middle of it was the perfect print of the hoof of the High Cow. I looked at it for a long time. Then I knelt down and in the centre, in the hoof print, I laid the silver sixpence that I had saved to make a wish on the Pin Tree. And there in that hoof I made my wish.